To my love who was my inspiration
to write this book Angelika.

You are my muse.

Introduction

I have always been a fan of Harry Potter. My girlfriend Angelika and I have spent countless hours watching the movies, as well as reading the books together. Angelika had always enjoyed pretending to be Hermione and would cast spells on me for fun. This was so much so that, during the Christmas of 2016, I thought it would be a fun gift to buy Angelika a wand and spellbook.

I began looking online and after many long Google searches I was unable to find a quality spellbook. I was looking for a spell book that contained all the spells, spell pronunciation and wand movements. I came to the conclusion that the only way to obtain the perfect spellbook would be if I were to make it myself. This book is the result of that effort.

In order to keep you, and others from experiencing the same frustration I went through I have decided to share this with you.

The Unofficial Harry Potter Spellbook: Wizard Training contains everything you need to channel your inner Hogwarts student. This edition includes spell names, pronunciation, wand movements, as well as other mentionable notes where deemed appropriate.

I have included all the spells from the Harry Potter universe whether they be from the LEGO video games, the movies or J.K Rowling's original work. It is a combination of all these elements that will provide you with what I consider to be a truly complete Harry Potter spellbook.

I hope this book will provide you with that much needed piece to complete your Harry Potter collection. So break out your wand and unleash the magic contained within The Unofficial Harry Potter Spellbook: Wizard Training.

     —Author Michael Gonzalez

A

Aberto

Spell Type: Charm

Pronunciation: Uh-bare-toe

A spell presumably used to open objects such as doors or windows.

Accio

Spell Type: Charm

Pronunciation: Various suggestions have been made, including: (AK-ee-oh) or (AK-see-oh)- According to the film, (AS -see-oh)- US according to the audio book.

This charm summons an object to the caster, potentially over a significant distance.

Aguamenti

Spell Type: Charm

Pronunciation: AH-gwah-MEN-tee

Produces a fountain or jet of water from the wand tip.

Alarte Ascendare

Spell Type: Charm

Pronunciation: A-LAR-tey ah-SEN-deh-rey

Shoots the target high into the air.

Alohomora

Spell Type: Charm

Pronunciation: al-LOH-ha-MOHR-ah

Used to open and unlock doors; it can unseal doors upon which the Locking Spell has been cast, although it is possible to bewitch doors to resist the spell.

Anapneo

Spell Type: Healing Spell

Pronunciation: ah-NAP-nee-oh

Clears the target's airway, should they find it blocked.

Anteoculatia

Spell Type: Hex

Pronunciation: AN-tea-oh-cuh-LAY-chee-a

Anteoculatia is a hex which turns a person's hair into antlers.

Aparecium

Spell Type: Charm

Pronunciation: AH-par-EE-see-um

This spell is used to reverse concealing charms, and can presumably render invisible ink visible. It is covered in a rather old spellbook. It may be related to Specialis Revelio.

Aqua Eructo

Spell Type: Charm

Pronunciation: A-kwa ee-RUCK-toh

This spell is used to create, and control, a jet of clear water from the tip of the wand; it is probably related to Aquamenti. Used multiple times to extinguish fires in 1994.

Arania Exumai

Spell Type: Spell

Pronunciation: ah-RAHN-ee-a EKS-su-may

This spell is used to blast away Acromantulas and, presumably, all other arachnids. Harry uses this spell in The Forbidden Forest to defend he and his friend from some spiders that are attacking them. He learned the spell from a diary, who attempted to use it in a memory.

Arresto Momentum

Spell Type: Charm

Pronunciation: ah-REST-oh mo-MEN-tum

Used to decrease the velocity of a moving target; it should be noted that it can be used on multiple targets, as well as on the caster himself. Used by Dumbledore to save one of his students from a fall in 1993; Hermione Granger used it, to little effect, in 1998 to cushion an otherwise deadly fall.

Ascendio

Spell Type: Charm
Pronunciation: ah-SEN-dee-oh
Lifts the caster high into the air.

Avada Kedavra

Spell Type: Curse
Pronunciation: ah-VAH-dah keh-DAV-rah

Causes instant death to the victim wherever it hits on the body, is accompanied by a flash of green light and a rushing noise

Avifors

Spell Type: Transfiguration
Pronunciation: AH-vi-fors
Transforms the target into a bird. Used multiple times throughout the video games.

Avis

Spell Type: Charm
Pronunciation: AH-viss

Conjures a flock of birds from the tip of the wand; when used in conjunction with Oppugno, it can be used offensively.

B

Baubillious

Spell Type: Charm

Pronunciation: baw—BILL—ee—us

The exact effects of the spell are unknown, though it presumably is of damaging nature and it produces a bolt of white light from the tip of the wand.

Bombarda

Spell Type: Charm

Pronunciation: bom—BAR—dah

Provokes a small explosion.

Bombarda Maxima

Spell Type: Charm
Pronunciation: BOM-bar-dah MAX-ih-mah

Creates a large explosion capable of removing entire walls.
A more advanced and more powerful form of Bombarda.

Brackium Emendo

Spell Type: Charm
Pronunciation: BRA-key-um ee-MEN-doh

If used correctly, it is claimed that this spell will heal
broken bones; this theory is supported by the etymology.

Calvario

Spell Type: Curse
Pronunciation: cal-VORE-ee-oh

This spell causes the victim's hair to fall out. In the LEGO Harry Potter: Years 5-7, the book Curses and Counter-Curses by Vindictus Viridian mentions this spell

Cantis

Spell Type: Jinx
Pronunciation: CAN-tiss

Causes the victim to burst uncontrollably into song. This spell can be bought in Wiseacre's Wizarding Equipment in LEGO Harry Potter: Years 5-7. Used by the Hogwarts professors to enchant suits of armour.

Carpe Retractum

Spell Type: Charm
Pronunciation: CAR-pay ruh-TRACK-tum

Produces a supernatural rope from the caster's wand, which will pull a target toward the caster.

Cave Inimicum

Spell Type: Charm
Pronunciation: KAH-way ih-NIH-mih-kum

Based on the etymology, it may warn the caster of any approaching enemies, similar to a Caterwauling Charm.

Cistem Aperio

Spell Type: Charm
Pronunciation: SIS-tem uh-PE-ree-o

Opens chests and boxes.

Colloportus

Spell Type: Charm
Pronunciation: cul-loh-POR-tus

Locks doors, and presumably all things that can be locked; it is unknown whether the counterspell is required, or if a key could open it.

Note: This spell can easily be countered with Alohomora.

Colloshoo

Spell Type: Hex
Pronunciation: cul-loh-SHOE

Adheres the victim's shoes to the ground with some sort of adhesive ectoplasm.

Colovaria

Spell Type: Charm
Pronunciation: co-loh-VA-riah

Changes the target's colour.

Confringo

Spell Type: Curse
Pronunciation: kon-FRING-goh

Causes anything that the spell comes into contact with to explode, and presumably thereafter burst into flame.

Note: This spell seems to use heat for its explosion, while Expulso uses pressure instead.

Confundo

Spell Type: Charm
Pronunciation: con-FUN-doh

Causes the victim to become confused and befuddled.

Crinus Muto

Spell Type: Transfiguration
Pronunciation: CREE-nus MYOO-toh

This spell can change the colour and style of ones hair. In
the Harry Potter Lego video games.

Note: This maybe be the spell
that causes Harry to turn his
eyebrow yellow in 1996.

Crucio

Spell Type: Curse
Pronunciation: KROO-shea-oh

Inflicts intense pain on the recipient of the curse; the
pain is described as having hot knives being driven into
the victim. It cannot be cast successfully by a person
who is doing so out of pure spite or anger; one must feel
a true desire to cause the victim pain.

D

Defodio

Spell Type: Charm
Pronunciation: deh-FOH-dee-oh

This spell allows the caster to gouge large chunks out of the target.

Deletrius

Spell Type: Charm
Pronunciation: deh-LEE-tree-us

Disintegrates something

Densaugeo

Spell Type: Hex

Pronunciation: den-SAW-jee-oh

This hex causes the victim's teeth to grow rapidly, but can also be used to restore lost teeth, as proven when Ted Tonks did so in 1997 for Harry Potter.

Depulso

Spell Type: Charm

Pronunciation: deh-PUL-soh

This spell is used to make the target fly toward a specific location; it is the opposite of the summoning charm.

Descendo

Spell Type: Charm

Pronunciation: deh-SEN-doh

Causes the target to move downwards.

Deprimo

Spell Type: Charm

Pronunciation: DEE-prih-moh

This spell places immense downward pressure on the target, which may result in the violent fracturing of said target.

Diffindo

Spell Type: Charm

Pronunciation: dih–FIN–doh

Rips, tears, shreds, or otherwise physically damages the target.

Diminuendo

Spell Type: Charm

Pronunciation: dim–in–YEW–en–DOUGH

Forces the target to shrink.

Dissendium

Spell Type: Charm

Pronunciation: dih–SEN–dee–um

Although the only known canonical effect is to open secret passageways, it's possible, based on its use in 1997, that it opens things in general.

Draconifors

Spell Type: Transfiguration

Pronunciation: drah–KOH–nih–fors

Transforms the target into a dragon.

Ducklifors

Spell Type: Transfiguration
Pronunciation: DUCK-lih-fors

Transforms the target into a duck.

Duro

Spell Type: Transfiguration
Pronunciation: DOO-roh

This charm transforms the target into solid stone.

E

Ebublio

Spell Type: Jinx

Pronunciation: ee-BUB-lee-oh

Causes the victim to inflate and explode into hundreds
of bubbles; it can only be cast if an ally is using Aqua
Eructo on the victim simultaneously.

Engorgio

Spell Type: Charm

Pronunciation: en-GOR-jee-oh

Causes the target to swell in physical size.

Engorgio Skullus

Spell Type: Hex

Pronunciation: in-GORE-jee-oh SKUH-las

This hex causes the victim's skull to swell disproportionately; this spell may be a variation of the Engorgement Charm, as they share the first word of the incantation. Its countercurse is Redactum Skullus.

Entomorphis

Spell Type: Jinx

Pronunciation: en-TOE-morph-is

This hex is used to transform the target into an insectoid for a short time; it can be bought at Wiseacre's Wizarding Equipment in Diagon Alley.

Episkey

Spell Type: Healing Spell

Pronunciation: ee-PISS-key

Used to heal relatively minor injuries, such as broken bones and cartilage.

Epoximise

Spell Type: Transfiguration

Pronunciation: ee-POX-i-mise

Adheres one object to another, similarly to if they had been glued together.

Erecto

Spell Type: Charm

Pronunciation: eh-RECK-toh

Used to erect a tent or other structure.

Evanesce

Spell Type: Transfiguration

Pronunciation: ev-an-ES-key

Vanishes the target

Evanesco

Spell Type: Transfiguration

Pronunciation: ev-an-ES-koh

Vanishes the target; the best description of what happens to it is that it goes "into non-being, which is to say, everything".

Everte Statum

Spell Type: Spell

Pronunciation: ee-VER-tay STAH-tum

Throws the victim backward, similarly to if they'd been thrown.

Expecto Patronum

Spell Type: Charm

Pronunciation: ecks–PECK–toh pah–TROH–numb

This charm is a defensive spell which will conjure a spirit-like incarnation of their positive emotions to defend against dark creatures; it can also send messages to other witches or wizards.

Expelliarmus

Spell Type: Charm

Pronunciation: ex–PELL–ee–ARE–muss

Causes whatever the victim is holding to fly away, knocks out an opponent if used too forcefully. Harry Potter's special spell.

Expulso

Spell Type: Curse

Pronunciation: ecks–PUHL–soh

Provokes an explosion, unique in that it uses pressure to do so as opposed to heat.

F

Ferula

Spell Type: Healing Spell

Pronunciation: feh-ROO-lah

Creates a bandage and a splint.

Fianto Duri

Spell Type: Charm

Pronunciation: fee-AN-toh DOO-ree

A defensive charm which, based on the etymology, strengthens shield spells, and perhaps objects in general, in a similar way to Duro.

Finite/Finite Incantatem

Spell Type: Counter-spell

Pronunciation: fi-NEE-tay / fi-NEE-tay in-can-TAH-tem

Terminates all spell effects in the vicinity of the caster.

Flagrate

Spell Type: Curse

Pronunciation: fluh-GRAH-tay

Produces fiery marks which can be used to write.
Tom Riddle used this spell to write his name; Hermione
Granger used it three years later to mark some doors.

Flipendo

Spell Type: Jinx

Pronunciation: flih-PEN-doh

Pushes the target, knocks out weaker enemies. Taught in
Defence Against the Dark Arts, used in every video game
thereafter until the third one. Not used in the books or
films.

Flipendo Duo

Spell Type: Jinx

Pronunciation: flih–PEN–doh DOO–oh

A more powerful version of Flipendo.

Flipendo Tria

Spell Type: Jinx

Pronunciation: flih–PEN–doh TREE–ah

A more powerful version of Flipendo Duo; it is said to resemble a miniature tornado.

Fumos

Spell Type: Charm

Used to produce a defensive cloud of dark grey smoke. This spell, used in 1993, is covered in The Dark Forces: A Guide to Self-Protection.

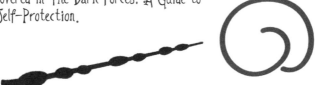

Fumos Duo

Spell Type: Charm

A more powerful version of Fumos.

Furnunculus

Spell Type: Jinx
Pronunciation: fer-NUN-kyoo-luss

Covers the target in boils (or pimples).

G

Geminio

Spell Type: Curse

Pronunciation: jeh—MIH—nee—oh

Creates an identical, useless copy of the target

Glacius

Spell Type: Charm

Pronunciation: GLAY—shuss

Transforms the target into solid albeit normal ice. Used in the video games. Never used in the books or films.

Glacius Duo

Spell Type: Charm

Pronunciation: GLAY-shuss DOO-oh

A more powerful version of Glacius.

Glacius Tria

Spell Type: Charm

Pronunciation: GLAY-shuss TREE-ah

A more powerful version of Glacius Duo.

Glisseo

Spell Type: Charm

Pronunciation: GLISS-ee-oh

Causes the steps on a stairway to flatten into a slide.

Harmonia Nectere Passus

Spell Type: Charm
Pronunciation: har-MOH-nee-a NECK-teh-ray PASS-us

Repairs a Vanishing Cabinet.

Herbifors

Spell Type: Transfiguration

This spell causes flowers to sprout from the victim.
It can be bought at Wiseacre's Wizarding Equipment.

Herbivicus

Spell Type: Charm
Pronunciation: her-BIV-i-cuss

Makes plants grow to full size instantaneously.

Homenum Revelio

Spell Type: Charm
Pronunciation: HOM—eh—num reh—VEH—lee—oh

Reveals human presence in the vicinity of the caster.

Notes: It can be used non-verbally;
Dumbledore does so to detect Harry
underneath his Invisibility Cloak.

I

Illegibilus

Spell Type: Charm
Pronunciation: i-lej-i-bill-us

Illegibilus is a spell that is used to render a text illegible.

Immobulus

Spell Type: Charm
Pronunciation: eem-o-bue-les

This spell causes flowers to sprout from the victim. It can be bought at Wiseacre's Wizarding Equipment.

Impedimenta

Spell Type: Jinx

Pronunciation: im-ped-ih-MEN-tah

This jinx is capable of tripping, freezing, binding,
knocking back and generally impeding the target's
progress towards the caster.

Imperio

Spell Type: Curse

Pronunciation: im-PEER-ee-oh

One of the three "Unforgivable Curses". Places the
subject in a dream-like state, in which he or she
is utterly subject to the will of the caster.

Impervius

Spell Type: Charm

Pronunciation: im-PUR-vee-us

This spell makes something repel (literally, become
impervious to) substances and outside forces including
water.

Impervius

Spell Type: Charm

Pronunciation: im–PUR–vee–us

This spell makes something repel (literally, become impervious to) substances and outside forces including water.

Inanimatus Conjurus

Spell Type: Transfiguration

Pronunciation: in–an–ih–MAH–tus CON–jur–us

It is a spell of unknown effect, most likely used to conjure an inanimate object.

Incarcerous

Spell Type: Conguration

Pronunciation: im–PUR–vee–us

This spell makes something repel (literally, become impervious to) substances and outside forces including water.

Incendio

Spell Type: Charm

Pronunciation: in–SEN–dee–oh

Produces fire.

Incendio Duo

Spell Type: Charm

Pronunciation: in-SEN-dee-oh DOO-oh

A stronger version of Incendio. It was in Harry Potter and the Chamber of Secrets.

Incendio Tria

Spell Type: Charm

Pronunciation: in-SEN-dee-oh TREE-ah

An improvement over both Incendio and Incendio Duo. It was seen in multiple video games

Inflatus

Spell Type: Charm

Pronunciation: in-FLAY-tus

Inflates objects (living or dead). One of the secondary spells in Harry Potter and the Goblet of Fire (video game) or possibly in "Harry Potter and the Prisoner of Azkaban (film).

Informous

Spell Type: Charm

Pronunciation: in-FOR-m-es

Informous is a spell that is used to complete one's Folio Bruti. A page with a brief description (including weaknesses and strengths) of the charmed creature is added to the caster's Folio Bruti. This was seen in the video game version of Harry Potter and the Chamber of Secrets.

L

Lacarnum Inflamarae

Spell Type: Charm
Pronunciation: la–CAR–num in–fla–MA–ray

It sends a ball of fire from the wand.

Langlock

Spell Type: Jinx
Pronunciation: LANG–lock

Glues the subject's tongue to the roof of
their mouth. Created by Severus Snape.

Lapifors

Spell Type: Transfiguration
Pronunciation: LAP-ih-forz

Turns small objects into real rabbits. Used by Hermione in the Harry Potter and the Prisoner of Azkaban and Harry Potter and the Goblet of Fire video games.

Legilimens

Spell Type: Charm
Pronunciation: Le-JIL-ih-mens

Allows the caster to delve into the mind of the victim, allowing the caster to see the memories, thoughts, and emotions of the victim.

Levicorpus

Spell Type: Jinx
Pronunciation: lev-ee-COR-pus

The victim is dangled upside-down by their ankles, sometimes accompanied by a flash of light (this may be a variant of the spell).

Liberacorpus

Spell Type: Counter-Jinx
Pronunciation: LIB-er-ah-cor-pus

Counteracts Levicorpus.

Locomotor

Spell Type: Charm

Pronunciation: LOH-koh-moh-tor

The spell is always used with the name of a target, at which the wand is pointed (e.g. "Locomotor Trunk!"). The spell causes the named object to rise in the air and move around at the will of the caster.

Locomotor Mortis

Spell Type: Curse

Pronunciation: LOH-koh-moh-tor MOR-tis

Locks the legs together, preventing the victim from moving the legs in any fashion.

Locomotor Wibbly

Spell Type: Curse

Pronunciation: loh-koh-MOH-tor WIB-lee

Causes the victim's legs to collapse.

Lumos

Spell Type: Charm

Pronunciation: LOO-mos

Creates a narrow beam of light that shines from the wand's tip, like a torch.

Lumos Duo

Spell Type: Charm

Pronunciation: LOO-mos DOO-oh

Creates an intense beam of light that projects from the wand's tip and can lock-on to various targets, turn hinkypunks solid and cause ghouls to retreat. Learned and used by Ron in the video game adaptation of Harry Potter and the Prisoner of Azkaban.

Lumos Maxima

Spell Type: Charm

Pronunciation: LOO-mos Ma-cks-ima

Shoots a ball of light at the place pointed, if the Wand is swung. First practised by Harry in the home of the Dursleys, then used by Dumbledore to light up the cave of the Horcrux.

Lumos Solem

Spell Type: Charm

Pronunciation: LOO-mos SO-lem

Creates a powerful ray of light as bright as the sun.

M

Magicus Extremos

Spell Type: Charm

Seen only in the video games, this simply makes all spells more powerful for a limited period of time. Used in Harry Potter and the Goblet of Fire (video game).

Melofors

Spell Type: Jinx

Encases the target's head in a pumpkin. Used in PoA game, GoF game, Harry Potter and the Order of the Phoenix, LEGO Harry Potter: Years 1-4/5-7.

Meteolojinx Recanto

Spell Type: Counter-Charm

Pronunciation: mee-tee-OH-loh-jinks reh-CAN-toh.

Presumably causes weather effects caused by jinxes to cease.

Mimblewimble

Spell Type: Curse

Pronunciation: MIM-bull-WIM-bull

A curse which prevents certain information from being revealed by the individual upon whom the spell is placed. The curse manifests itself by causing the tongue to temporarily curl backwards upon itself.

Mobiliarbus

Spell Type: Charm

Pronunciation: MO-bil-ee-AR-bus

Levitates and moves an object.

Mobilicorpus

Spell Type: Charm

Pronunciation: MO-bil-ee-COR-pus

Levitates and moves bodies.

Morsmordre

Spell Type: Dark Mark

Pronunciation: morz–MOR–duh,
morz–MOHR–dah, morz–MOR–drah

Conjures the Dark Mark, which
is the sign of the Death Eaters.

Muffliato

Spell Type: Curse

Pronunciation: muf–lee–AH–to

A curse which prevents certain information from
being revealed by the individual upon whom the spell
is placed. The curse manifests itself by causing the
tongue to temporarily curl backwards upon itself.

Multicorfors

Spell Type: Transfiguration

Pronunciation: mull–tee–COR–fors

Multicorfors is a charm used to change the colour of one's
clothing. It can be bought at Wiseacre's Wizarding Equipment
in Diagon Alley in LEGO Harry Potter: Years 1-4.

N

Nox

Spell Type: Charm

Pronunciation: Nocks

Turns off the light produced by Lumos. In 1994, Harry Potter and Hermione Granger used this spell to turn off their wand-lights in the Shrieking Shack.

O

Oculus Reparo

Spell Type: Charm

Mends eyeglasses.

Notes: This spell is a variation of Reparo.

Obliviate

Spell Type: Charm

Pronunciation: oh-BLI-vee-ate

Used to hide a memory of a particular event. Hermione Granger used this spell to wipe her parents memories in 1997.

Obscuro

Spell Type: Conjuration

Pronunciation: ob–SK(Y)OOR–oh

Causes a blindfold to appear over the victim's eyes, obstructing their view of their surroundings.

Oppugno

Spell Type: Jinx

Pronunciation: oh–PUG–noh

Apparently causes animals or beings of lesser intelligence to attack.

Orbis

Spell Type: Jinx

Pronunciation: OR–biss

Sucks the target into the ground.

Orchideous

Spell Type: Conjuration

Makes a bouquet of flowers appear out of the caster's wand.

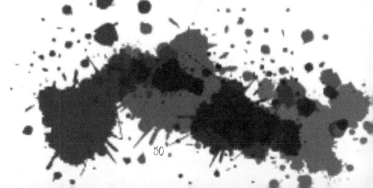

P

Pack

Spell Type: Charm

Pronunciation: pak

Packs a trunk, or perhaps any luggage. Used in Harry Potter and the Prisoner of Azkaban by Remus Lupin in his office, and in Harry Potter and the Order of the Phoenix by Nymphadora Tonks, once verbally and again non-verbally.

Partis Temporus

Spell Type: Charm

Pronunciation: PAR-tis temp-OAR-us

Creates a temporary gap through protective magical barriers. Used by Albus Dumbledore in the Crystal Cave in the film adaptation of Harry Potter and the Half-Blood Prince.

Periculum

Spell Type: Charm

Pronunciation: pur—ICK—you—lum

Creates red sparks/flares to shoot from the users wand.

Peskipiksi Pesternomi

Spell Type: Charm

Pronunciation: PES—key PIX—ee PES—ter NO—mee

The one time it was used, it had absolutely no effect. Used by Lockhart to attempt to remove Cornish Pixies.

Petrificus Totalus

Spell Type: Curse

Pronunciation: pe—TRI—fi—cus to—TAH—lus

Used to temporarily bind the victim's body in a position much like that of a soldier at attention; the victim will usually fall to the ground.

Piertotum Locomotor

Spell Type: Charm

Pronunciation: pee-ayr-TOH-tum (or peer-TOH-tum) loh-koh-MOH-tor

In the Battle of Hogwarts, Professor McGonagall used this spell to animate the suits of armour and statues within Hogwarts, to defend the castle.

Point Me

Spell Type: Spell

Pronunciation: English phrase

Causes the caster's wand to act as a compass, and point North.

Portus

Spell Type: Charm

Pronunciation: POR-tus

Turns an object into a port-key

Prior Incantato

Spell Type: Charm

Pronunciation: pri-OR in-can-TAH-toh

Causes the echo (a shadow or image) of the last spell cast by a wand to emanate from it. Used by Amos Diggory in 1994 to discover the last spell cast by Harry's wand after it was found in the hands of Winky, a house-elf.

Protego

Spell Type: Charm

Pronunciation: pro-TAY-goh

The Shield Charm causes minor to moderate jinxes, curses, and hexes to rebound upon the attacker, protecting the caster.

Protego Horribilis

Spell Type: Charm

Pronunciation: pro-TAY-goh horr-uh-BIHL-ihs

A powerful shield charm against dark magic. Cast by Professor Flitwick in an attempt to strengthen the castle's defences in the Battle of Hogwarts.

Protego Maxima

Spell Type: Charm

Pronunciation: pro-TAY-goh MAX-ee-Ma

A powerful shield charm against dark magic. A stronger and bigger version of Protego, especially when combined with other wizards casting it at the same time. Was so powerful that it could also disintegrate people that came too close and tried to enter it.

Protego Totalum

Spell Type: Charm

Pronunciation: pro-TAY-goh prah-TEH-go toh-TAH-lum

Casts a shield charm over a small area that will
not let anything pass through, except for the
Unforgivable Curses: Avada Kedavra, Imperio and
Crucio.

Q

Quietus

Spell Type: Charm
Pronunciation: KWIY-uh-tus

Makes a magically magnified voice return to normal. A counter to Sonorus

R

Redactum Skullus

Spell Type: Hex

Pronunciation: red-AK-tum SKULL-us

Redactum Skullus is a hex that shrinks the target's head. It is the counter-spell to Engorgio Skullus.

Reducio

Spell Type: Charm

Pronunciation: re-DOO-see-oh

Makes an enlarged object smaller. Counter-charm to Engorgio.

Reducto

Spell Type: Curse

Pronunciation: re-DUK-toh

Breaks objects. In stronger
usages, disintegrates them.

Reparifors

Spell Type: Healing Spell

Reverts minor magically-induced ailments, such as paralysis
and poisoning.

Relashio

Spell Type: Jinx

Pronunciation: Re-LASH-ee-oh

A spell used to make the subject release
what ever it is holding or binding.

Rennervate

Spell Type: Charm

Pronunciation: ree-nur-VAH-tay, REN-ur-vayt

Revives a stunned person.

Reparifarge

Spell Type: Untransfiguration

Pronunciation: reh—PAH—ree—fahj

Used to reverse unsuccessful transformations. Seen only thus far in A Beginner's Guide to Transfiguration on Pottermore.

Reparo

Spell Type: Charm

Pronunciation: reh—PAH—roh

Used to repair objects.

Repello Muggletum

Spell Type: Untransfiguration

Pronunciation: reh—PELL—loh MUG—ul—tum, MUGG—gleh—tum, mugg—GLEE—tum

Keeps Muggles away from wizarding places by causing them to remember important meetings they missed and to cause the Muggles in question to forget what they were doing.

Repello Inimicum

Spell Type: Charm

Pronunciation: re-PEH-lloh ee-nee-MEE-cum

Disintegrates the persons entering this charm.

Revelio

Spell Type: Charm

Pronunciation: reh-VEL-ee-oh

Reveals hidden objects

Rictusempra

Spell Type: Charm

Pronunciation: ric-tuhs-SEM-pra

Causes an extreme tickling sensation that, in the case of Draco Malfoy, made him drop to the floor laughing.

Riddikulus

Spell Type: Charm

Pronunciation: ri-di-KULL-lis

A spell used when fighting a Boggart, "Riddikulus" forces the Boggart to take the appearance of an object the caster is focusing on.

S

Salvio Hexia

Spell Type: Hex

Pronunciation: SAL-vee-oh HECKS-ee-ah

Unknown, as it was one of several spells that were used to help strengthen Harry's camp-site, and had no seen effects.

Scourgify

Spell Type: Charm

Pronunciation: SKUR-jih-fiy

Used to clean something.

Sectumsempra

Spell Type: Curse

Pronunciation: sec-tum-SEMP-rah

A dark spell that creates large, blood-oozing gashes on the subject as if said subject had been "slashed by a sword". Invented by Severus Snape.

Serpensortia

Spell Type: Transfiguration

Pronunciation: ser-pen-SOR-shah, SER-pehn-SOR-tee-ah

Conjures a serpent from the spell-caster's wand.

Silencio

Spell Type: Charm

Pronunciation: sih-LEN-see-oh

Makes something silent.

Skurge

Spell Type: Charm

Pronunciation: SKUR-je

Cleans up ectoplasm, the slime-like residue left by certain ghosts. The spell manifests as a blast of greenish suds.

Slugulus Eructo

Spell Type: Charm

A jet of green light strikes the victim, who then vomits slugs for ten minutes. The sizes of the vomited slugs decrease with time.

Sonorus

Spell Type: Charm

Pronunciation: soh-NOHR-uhs

Magnifies the spell caster's voice when one's wand is pointing to the side of the caster's neck.

Specialis Revelio

Spell Type: Charm

Pronunciation: speh-see-AH-LIS reh-VEL-ee-oh

Apparently causes an object to show its hidden secrets or magical properties.

Spongify

Spell Type: Charm

Pronunciation: spun-JIH-fy

Softens the target.

Steleus

Spell Type: Hex

Pronunciation: STÉ-lee-us

A hex that causes the victim to sneeze for a short period of time. This spell is used in duellingto distract the opponent. It is only seen in Harry Potter and the Prisoner of Azkaban (video game).

Stupefy

Spell Type: Charm

Pronunciation: STOO-puh-fye

Stuns victim. If used too forcefully, it will put the victim in an unconscious state.

T

Tarantallegra

Spell Type: Jinx

Pronunciation: tuh-RAHN-tuh-LEHG-rah

Makes victim's legs dance uncontrollably
(recalling the tarantella dance).

Tentaclifors

Spell Type: Transfiguration-Jinx

Transfigures the target's head
into a tentacle.

Tergeo

Spell Type: Charm

Pronunciation: TUR-jee-oh

Siphons liquid

Titillando

Spell Type: Hex

Tickles and weakens. Harry Potter Trading Card Game, later seen in spells/duels on Pottermore

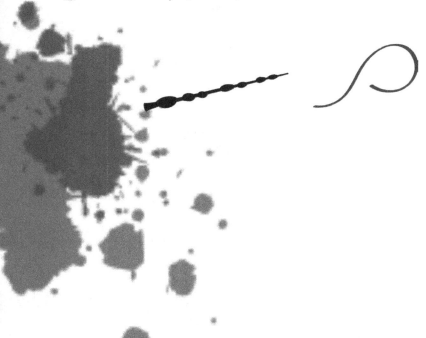

V

Ventus

Spell Type: Jinx

Pronunciation: ven–TUS

A strong blast of wind is shot from the end of the wand,
used to push objects out of the way. Used in the video
game version of Harry Potter and the Goblet of Fire.

Ventus Duo

Spell Type: Jinx

A stronger version of the Ventus
Jinx

Vera Verto

Spell Type: Transfiguration

Pronunciation: vair-uh-VAIR-toh

Turn animals to water goblets.

Verdillious

Spell Type: Charm

Pronunciation: ver-DILL-ee-us

A spell used to shoot green sparks from the end of the wand. Seen in the trading card game.

Verdimillious

Spell Type: Charm

Pronunciation: VERD-dee-MILL-lee-us

A spell that shoots green sparks at the end of the wand.

Verdimillious Duo

Spell Type: Charm

Pronunciation: VERD-dee-MILL-lee-us DUH-oh

A more powerful version of Verdimillious.

Vipera Evanesca

Spell Type: Untransfiguration

Pronunciation: IYP-er-uh ehv-uhn-EHS-kuh

Counter Spell for Serpensortia. Seems not to merely "Vanish", but causes the snake to smoulder from head and tail until it is reduced to a pile of ashes.

Vulnera Sanentur

Spell Type: Healing-Spell

Pronunciation: vul-nur-ah sahn-en-tur

Causes wounds and gashes to heal up and any blood to return to the victim.

W

Waddiwasi

Spell Type: Charm

Pronunciation: wah-dee-WAH-see

Appears to launch small objects through the air, though it was only ever used on a wad of chewing gum.

Wingardium Leviosa

Spell Type: Charm

Pronunciation: win-GAR-dee-um lev-ee-OH-sa

Levitates, moves and manipulates the target(similar to telekinesis); the wand motion is described as "swish and flick".

Other Spells & Incantations

Age Line

Spell Type: Charm

Creates a thin, shimmering golden line around the target that is impassable by those below a set age. It seems that ageing potions are useless against the line, and it appears that the lines functions on either calendar or mental age.

Albus Dumbledore's Forceful Spell

This spell was, supposedly, quite powerful as when it was cast, the opponent was forced to conjure a silver shield to deflect it. This incantation was used only once throughout the series, and that was by Dumbledore in the Ministry of Magic, immediately following the Battle of the Department of Mysteries on 17 June, 1996, while he duelled Voldemort.

Anti-Jinx

Spell Type: Counter Spell

Prevents the effects of a jinx over one target object or animal. In the summer of 1995, Arthur Weasley was required to perform an antijinx on a regurgitating toilet.

Anti-Cheating Spell

Spell Type: Charm

Cast on parchment and quills to prevent the writer from cheating while writing answers. Used near exam times at Hogwarts in at least 1991 and 1995.

Anti-Disapparition Jinx

Spell Type: Jinx

Used to prevent Disapparating in an area for a time; presumably used to trap an enemy in an area, is probably related to the Anti-Apparition Charm. Used by Albus Dumbledore to trap some Death Eaters in the Department of Mysteries in 1996. Also mentioned that nobody can disapparate from Hogwarts; it is due to this jinx.

Antonin Dolohov's Curse

Spell Type: Curse

Based on what is seen of the effects, it is presumed to be a nearly lethal spell used to cause severe internal injury. Used by Antonin Dolohov during the Battle of the Department of Mysteries twice; once on Hermione Granger (which incapacitated her instantly and required her to take ten potions a day for some time) and again, ineffectively, on Harry Potter.

Arrow shooting Spell

Spell Type: Conjuration

Fires arrows from the caster's wand. The spell used to be used by Appleby Arrows supporters at Quidditch matches to show their support for their teams; however, the British and Irish Quidditch League banned the use of the spell at matches when referee Nugent Potts was pierced through the nose with a stray arrow in 1894.

Babbling Curse

Spell Type: Curse

Although this spell is not fully understood, it is generally presumed to force a person to babble whenever they speak; it is possibly, for this reason, related to the Tongue-Tying Curse. Although he was rather untrustworthy, it may not have occurred at all, but Lockhart says he cured a Transylvanian farmer of this affliction.

Bat-Bogey Hex

Spell Type: Hex

It is another spell that is not fully understood, but most people presume, based on clues from the text, that it grotesquely enlarges the target's bogies, gives them wings, and sets them attacking the target. Ginny Weasley was a noted practitioner of this spell, having used it at least thrice by her sixth year.

Bedazzling Hex

Spell Type: Hex

Though the exact effects are unknown, based on the name (and the fact that it is used in conjunction with a chameleon charm on certain cloaks, it is probably used to conceal a person or object. When Xenophilius Lovegood explains the concept of how the Cloak of Invisibility is the only thing that can make a person truly invisible, he mentions that most cloaks of that kind are made with this spell.

Bewitched Snowballs

Spell Type: Charm

Presumably causes snowballs to pelt themselves at the target.
Twice used by Fred and George Weasley; firstly on Professor
Quirrell's head, unwittingly striking Lord Voldemort in the face,
and then again four years later to attack the windows of
Gryffindor Tower.

Bluebell Flames

Spell Type: Charm

Conjures a quantity of waterproof blue flames that can be carried
around in a container, released, then "scooped" back therein. This
spell was a specialty of Hermione Granger's. She used it to save
Harry and Ron in 1991.

Bubble-Head Charm

Spell Type: Charm

Produces a large bubble of air around the head of the user; it is
commonly used as the supernatural equivalent of a breathing set.
Used by Cedric Diggory and Fleur Delacour in 1995; it was
used the next year by many students walking through the halls,
because of horrid odours made by various pranks played on Dolores
Umbridge.

Bubble-producing Spell

Spell Type: Charm

Produces a stream of multicoloured, non-bursting bubbles; there are two similar spells. Used by Professor Flitwick to decorate some trees; the bubbles in this instance were golden. Used the following year by Ron Weasley when he broke his wand; these bubbles were purple.

Cascading Jinx

Spell Type: Jinx

An offensive spell used to defeat multiple enemies. This spell was seen only in Harry Potter and the Deathly Hallows: Part 1 (video game).

Caterwauling Charm

Spell Type: Charm

Anyone entering the perimeter of this spell sets off a high-pitched shriek. This spell may be related to the Intruder Charm. This spell was cast by the Death Eaters over Hogsmeade Wizarding Village to protect against intruders in 1998.

Cauldron to Sieve

Spell Type: Transfiguration

Transforms cauldrons, and presumably all pots and containers of that sort, into sieves. This spell was only seen in the Harry Potter Trading Card Game.

Cheering Charm

Spell Type: Charm

Causes the person upon whom the spell is cast to become
contented and happy, though heavy-handedness with it causes
the victim to break into an uncontrollable laughing fit. Taught to
third-year charms classes, part of the written O.W.L. The spell
was invented by Felix Summerbee.

Conjunctivitis Curse

Spell Type: Curse

Due to the name (conjunctivitis is another word for "pink eye",
a disease which forms a scabby inflammation over the eye), it is
presumed this curse causes great pain to the victim's eyes.

Cornflake Skin Spell

Spell Type: Unknown

This spell causes the victim's skin to appear as though it was
coated in cornflakes. In 1996, an unnamed student went to
the hospital for treatment after he was hit with it, which
was presumably done in retaliation for the Inquisitorial Squad's
recent behaviour.

Cracker Jinx

Spell Type: Jinx

This spell is used to conjure exploding wizard crackers; it can
be used in duelling to harm the opponent, but the force of the
explosion may also affect the caster.

Cribbing Spell

Spell Type: Jinx

This spell, which may possibly be a charm, is used to assist the caster in cheating on written papers, tests, and exams. It is possible that these spells can negate anti-cheating spells. In 1991, an unnamed Slytherin student asked his fellow students whether any of them knew any good cribbing spells.

Cushioning Charm

Spell Type: Charm

Produces an invisible cushion over the target, is used primarily in the manufacturing of broomsticks. Used by Hermione Granger to cushion her, Harry, and Ron's fall in Gringotts Wizard Bank in 1998.

Disillusionment Charm

Spell Type: Charm

Causes the target to blend seamlessly in with its surroundings, like a chameleon. Used and mentioned multiple times from 1995 onward.

Drought Charm

Spell Type: Charm

Causes puddles and ponds to dry up. Though not powerful enough to drain a body of water like a lake. Mentioned by Ronald Weasley in 1994 when Harry was getting ready for the Second Task of The Triwizard Tournament.

Ears to Kumquats

Spell Type: Transfiguration

This spell transforms the victim's ears into kumquats. In 1995, Luna Lovegood read The Quibbler upside down in order to reveal the secret charm, written in Ancient Runes.

Ear-shrivelling Curse

Spell Type: Curse

Causes the target's ears to shrivel up. Sometime between 1989 and 1994, Bill Weasley's pen-friend sent him a hat with this curse on it.

Entrail-Expelling Curse

Spell Type: Curse

Presumably causes the victim's insides to be ejected from the body, though due to the fact that a portrait of its inventor was hung in a hospital, it is possible this spell's effect is entirely different.

Extinguishing Spell

Spell Type: Spell

Puts out fires. Charlie Weasley and his friends would use this spell should something go wrong in the tournament.

Eye of rabbit, harp string hum, turn this water into rum

Spell Type: Transfiguration

Turns water into rum. Seamus Finnigan tried to cast it in 1991, and, in his first attempt, he managed to make "weak tea," before causing an explosion.

Feather-light Charm

Spell Type: Charm

Makes something lightweight. Harry Potter contemplated using this in 1993 to lighten his trunk so that he could carry it by broom to Gringotts, though he decided against it.

Notes: This charm may have been cast by Hermione Granger on her beaded bag to make it easier to carry, considering the heavy objects within.

Fidelius Charm

Spell Type: Charm

A complex charm used to hide secret information within the soul of the charm's recipient, who is called a Secret-Keeper. The information is irretrievable unless the Secret-Keeper chooses to reveal it, and only the aforementioned person can do so.

Fiendfyre

Spell Type: Curse

Creates great spirits of fire which burn anything in its path, including nearly indestructable substances such as horcruxes. This fire is nearly impossible to control. Though there are numerous instances when it may have been used, it was only proven to have been used in 1998 by Vincent Crabbe, who was killed by it.

Finger-removing Jinx

Spell Type: Jinx

Removes a person's fingers. Gunhilda Kneen jinxed her husband with this spell.

Firestorm

Spell Type: Charm

Produces a ring of fire from the wand tip that can strike targets. Albus Dumbledore used this spell to rescue Harry from Inferi in 1997.

Flagrante Curse

Spell Type: Curse

Causes the cursed object to burn human skin when touched. The Lestrange Vault had this curse on it.

Flame-Freezing Charm
Spell Type: Charm

Causes fire to tickle those caught in it instead of burning them. Third year students wrote an essay on the use of this charm in medieval witch-burnings; Wendelin the Weird was burned forty-seven times.

Flying Charm
Spell Type: Charm

This spell is cast on broomsticks and flying carpets to allow them to fly. Draco Malfoy mentioned this spell when insulting Ron Weasley's broomstick, wondering why anyone would charm it.

Fur Spell
Spell Type: Charm

Causes fur to grow on the victim. Fred and George Weasley used this spell on each other.

Green Sparks
Spell Type: Charm

Shoots green sparks from the wand. Taught in Defence Against the Dark Arts

Gripping Charm

Spell Type: Charm

Helps someone grip something more effectively. Used on Quaffles to help Chasers carry them.

Hair-Thickening Charm

Spell Type: Charm

Thickens the victim's hair. Alicia Spinnet was hexed with this spell in 1996.

Hermione Granger's Jinx

Spell Type: Jinx

Causes a traitor to break out in boils spelling "SNEAK" on his or her forehead. Hermione Granger designed and placed this jinx on the parchment signed by all members of Dumbledore's Army. When Marietta Edgecombe betrayed the D.A. to Dolores Umbridge, the jinx was triggered.

Homing Spell

Spell Type: Spell

Offensive spells that follow their target with a constant speed after being cast.

Homonculous Charm

Spell Type: Charm

Tracks movement of every person in the mapped area. Used to create the Marauder's Map.

Homorphus Charm

Spell Type: Charm

Causes an Animagus or transfigured object to assume its normal shape.

Horton-Keitch Braking Charm

Spell Type: Charm

This spell was first used on the Comet 140 to prevent players from overshooting the goal posts and from flying off-sides. Mentioned in Quidditch Through the Ages as the charm that gave the Comet 140 an advantage over the Cleansweep.

Horcrux Curse

Spell Type: Curse

This spell allows a part of a wizard's soul to pass into an object, thereby making the object a Horcrux. One has to commit murder and take advantage of the soul's "splitting apart" by this supreme act of evil in order to be able to perform this spell, and it is probably very complex.

Notes: When J.K.Rowling was asked about what the steps are to create a Horcrux Rowling declined to answer, saying that "some things are better left unsaid".

Hot-Air Charm

Spell Type: Charm

Causes wand to emit hot air. Used by Hermione Granger in 1995 to dry off her robes. Also used shortly after to melt snow.

Hour-Reversal Charm

Spell Type: Charm

Reverses small amounts of time (up to five hours). Used to create Time-Turners, as mentioned by Professor Saul Croaker; this charm is highly unstable.

Hover Charm

Spell Type: Charm

Causes the target to float in mid-air for a brief period of time. Used by Dobby to levitate a cake.

Hurling Hex

Spell Type: Hex

Causes brooms to vibrate violently in the air and try to buck their rider off.

Imperturbable Charm

Spell Type: Charm

Makes objects such as doors impenetrable (by everything, including sounds and objects).

Jelly-Brain Jinx

Spell Type: Jinx

Presumably affects the target's mental processes. During the September 1999 riot that took place during the Puddlemere United/Holyhead Harpies Quidditch game, a lot of Harpy supporters were using this jinx.

Jelly-Fingers Curse

Spell Type: Curse

Causes the target's fingers to become almost jelly-like to make it uneasy for the victim to grasp objects.

Knee-Reversal Hex

Spell Type: Hex

Causes the victim's knees to appear on the opposite side of his/her legs. In Quidditch Through the Ages, Gertie Keddle uses this hex when a man playing an early form of Quidditch comes to retrieve his ball from her garden.

Leek Jinx

Spell Type: Jinx

Makes leeks sprout out of the target's ears. Used by a fighting Gryffindor fourth year and sixth year Slytherin before a Quidditch match in 1992.

Molly Weasley's Curse

Spell Type: Curse

Like the Avada Kedavra curse, it kills (or freezes) the victim. It turns the body grey/blue (or paler) while it turns to stone and then another twin jinx can blast the body into pieces. Molly Weasley used the curse after Bellatrix Lestrange attacked Ginny Weasley. Only used in the film version.

Obliteration Charm

Spell Type: Charm

Removes footprints.

Patented Daydream Charm

Spell Type: Charm

Gives the spell caster a highly-realistic 30-minute daydream. Side effects include mild drooling and a vacant expression.

Permanent Sticking Charm

Spell Type: Charm

Makes objects permanently stay in place.

Placement Charm

Spell Type: Charm

A charm which temporarily places an object upon a desired target. Mentioned in Fantastic Beasts and Where to Find Them.

Protean Charm

Spell Type: Charm

Causes copies of an object to be remotely affected by changes made to the original.

Purple Firecrackers

Spell Type: Charm

Causes purple firecrackers to shoot out from the tip of one's wand. On 31 October 1991, Albus Dumbledore used this spell to get the attention of panicking diners in the Great Hall when a troll was loose in the castle.

Pus-Squirting Hex

Spell Type: Hex

Causes yellowish goo to squirt from one's nose. Morfin Gaunt used this hex on Bob Ogden.

Refilling Charm

Spell Type: Charm

Refills whatever the caster points at with the drink originally in the container. Used in Harry Potter and the Half-Blood Prince, when Harry notices that Hagrid and Slughorn are running out of wine.

Rose Growth

Spell Type: Transfiguration

Causes rosebushes grow at an unusually fast pace. Harry Potter Trading Card Game

Rowboat Spell

Spell Type: Charm

A spell invented by Hagrid which propels row boats to a pre-set destination.

Scorching Spell

Spell Type: Spell

Produces dancing flames which presumably scorch the opponent. Professor McGonagall used this spell on Professor Snape in 1998.

Shield Penetration Spell

Spell Type: Spell

Presumably annihilates magical enchantments and shields.

Shooting Spell

Spell Type: Spell

Used to shoot objects. This spell was used by Harry Potter and Ronald Weasley in 1997 on their Horcrux huntin an attempt to catch a rabbit for food.

Smashing Spell

Spell Type: Spell

Produces explosions

Sonorous Charm

Spell Type: Charm

This charm emits a magnified roar from the tip of the wand. This noise disrupts all in its path, and can even be used to harm opponents.

Stealth Sensoring Spell

Spell Type: Spell

Detects those under magical disguise. In 1996, Professor Umbridge cast this around her office.

Stinging Hex

Spell Type: Hex

Produces a stinging sensation in the victim, resulting in angry red welts and occasionally the severe inflammation of the affected area.

Supersensory Charm

Spell Type: Charm

Presumably causes the caster to have enhanced senses, or to be able to sense things they would not normally sense.

Switching Spell

Spell Type: Tranfiguration

Causes two objects to be switched for one another. Harry contemplated using this spell against his dragon in the first task of the Triwizard Tournament.

Taboo

Spell Type: Jinx

A jinx which may be placed upon a word or a name, so that whenever that word is spoken, a magical disturbance is created which alerts the caster of the Taboo to the location of the speaker. Any protective enchantments in effect around the speaker are broken when the Tabooed word is spoken aloud.

Teleportation Spell

Spell Type: Jinx

Vanishes objects which then appear elsewhere. In 1996, Albus Dumbledore used this to transport Harry Potter's school supplies, clothes, and owl to the Burrow.

Toenail Growth Hex

Spell Type: Hex

Causes the toenails to grow at an extreme and uncontrollable rate.

Tooth-growing Spell

Spell Type: Hex

A spell that re-grows lost teeth. Ted Tonks used it to re-grow Harry Potter's tooth that he had lost during the Battle of the Seven Potters.

Transmogrifian Torture

Spell Type: Curse

Unknown effect upon victim; most likely extreme torture that can lead to death. Given the source, the Torture may not actually exist. Gilderoy Lockhart suggested that it was this curse that "killed" Mrs Norris after she was really found petrified on a torch bracket.

Trip Jinx
Spell Type: Jinx

A jinx to trip up or impede the target. Precise effects unknown.

Unbreakable Vow
Spell Type: Spell

Causes a vow taken by a witch or wizard to be inviolable; if they should break it, the consequence is death.

Unbreakable Charm
Spell Type: Charm

Kes something unbreakable.

Undetectable Extension Charm
Spell Type: Charm

Causes a container's capacity to be increased, without changing the object's appearance on the outside.

Washing Up Spell
Spell Type: Charm

Enchanted dirty dishes to wash themselves.